ANOTHER SET OF HANDS

A COLLECTION OF
SHORT DIACONAL STORIES

Rev. Mr. Tom Quinlan

Foreword by Deacon Ron Ansay

ALT PUBLISHING CO.

Published by Alt Publishing Co.
502 George St.
De Pere, WI 54115

Marketed and Distributed by:
Queue Productions
P.O. Box 1010
Conifer, CO 80433
Telephone 303-838-4391

The cover design is an enlargement of a lapel pin for deacons, used with permission of its designer, Bill Spellman of Blackhawk, Colorado.

Library of Congress Control Number: 00-0909850
ISBN 0-9615691-1-5
Manufactured in the United States of America.

deacontom@ctkevergreen.com

Contents

Dedication

This book is humbly dedicated to the memory
of the late Reverend Marcian T. O'Meara
of the Archdiocese of Denver, Colorado.
For almost 20 years, Father O'Meara was
the director of the permanent deacon
program, for the archdiocese. He took the
program and developed it into a nationally
recognized diaconal formation program.
For two years he was also my pastor.
For everything you have done for the
deacon program . . . thank you.

Foreword

Rev. Mr. Tom Quinlan is certainly a very talented and gifted man, as well as a world traveler. As one reads about the author, the pattern of God's Call and Vocation is apparent. A blending of all into the present moment which contains his marriage to Glenys, his fatherhood, his business life, his hobbies and his diaconal ministry. I am blessed to be a personal friend of Tom for many years and to observe the Holy Spirit alive in his multi-faceted life, he is truly an icon of Christ.

Like many expressions of ministry, the diaconate is certainly coming into its own as the vocation it truly is, one of the new vocations in the Church. Deacon Tom puts a face on the word "deacon" with his often humorous and yet spiritually sensitive short stories. His keen mind captures the moment and turns an ordinary event into a homily of life.

As a member of the married clergy in the Catholic Church, Deacon Tom brings a fresh look at the sacraments and other ministry stories. It appears that simplicity is the key factor and the depth simplicity can bring into any situation.

Enjoy Tom's stories and may they touch you as they have touched me. May all our Deacon brothers and Deacon wives be further inspired as they live this very special vocation of service to God's people. Thank you, Deacon Tom!

Deacon Ron Ansay
Diocese of Colorado Springs, Colorado

Acknowledgements

Very special thanks to my wife, the former Glenys Larson of Albion, Nebraska. I thank her for her encouragement, support and advice. Without her patience and insight this book would not have been possible.

I also want to thank everyone who read the manuscript, starting with my bishop, the Most Reverend Charles J. Chaput, O.F.M. Cap., the Archbishop of Denver. The Archbishop took my manuscript with him and read it on a recent plane trip. Fr. Christopher Renner, pastor of Christ the King Catholic Church in Evergreen, Colorado, and Fr. Eugene Bova, a retired priest of the Diocese of Bismarck, North Dakota, who lives down the road from me and is my Spiritual Director. Padre, as he likes to be called, and I share a special friendship, we are also both Amateur Radio "HAMS."

I also want to thank Cindy Craig of Evergreen, Colorado who for years has been my typist and edits all my rough copy; Dr. Robert Suding, a neighbor and friend for his computer expertise, as well as Phil Lauter of Conifer, who runs Rocky Mountain Non-Linear and was able to take the deacon lapel pin and prepare it for use on the cover. Another thank you goes out to Joan Sheehan, Principal of Our Lady of Lourdes Catholic School in Denver who also read my manuscript and gave me several suggestions and ideas. If I have forgotten anybody, I am sorry.

If you the reader are thinking about whether God is calling you to become a deacon and my stories have helped you, I am happy. If you just enjoyed my stories, I am happy.

They say the Irish are great story tellers. I hope my stories at least come up to the high water mark when the tide is in. The overall goal was to share my ministry with you, and to make you laugh, and to make you cry and also, to witness the presence of Jesus Christ in our lives.

If you would like to obtain additional copies
of Tom's book "Another Set of Hands"
send $9.95 in check or money order, postpaid to:

QUEUE PRODUCTIONS
BOX 1010
Conifer, CO 80433

My Call to the Diaconate

In 1977 I had absolutely no idea that I would be called to the diaconate. I was having a problem with God. I had a hard time accepting the fact that the deacon in our parish had recently died, having been ordained just a short time. I knew he had a hard time getting through the program and worked very hard. I thought it extremely unfair of God to call him home so soon after his ordination, and I was angry.

I used to attend daily Mass at Dyess AFB in Abilene, Texas every day at noon and sort of fell into reading the Old Testament and the Responsorial Psalm. One day I read the passage "For every worker in my vineyard that I call home, I will send a replacement." Right then and there I knew I was to be the replacement for the deacon who had recently died. I was so overwhelmed at what I had just read that I could not go on. I closed the book and walked to the first row and looked into the face of the dead deacon's widow and said to her, "Do you understand what I just read means that I am to be your late husband's replacement?" Tears filled my eyes and I could hardly see.

I walked back to where the priest was standing and simply said, "Father, I have been called to be a deacon." He read the Psalm and the Gospel and continued with Mass. After Mass, he suggested I contact the pastor of the Catholic Church we attended on Sundays and explain everything to him. I called and made an appointment and met with him and told him everything. He called the Chancery and talked with the bishop who wanted to meet me the following Saturday in San Angelo, Texas. My family and I made the trip and met with the bishop.

What an event that was. His name was Bishop Stephen Leven, and what a holy man he was, with a sense of humor to boot. After meeting with my wife and I and our two sons, he handed me a box of books and cassette tapes with instructions to go home and read them so as to catch up with the class that had been in session for two months. I was to be the absolute last member of the class. For the next two years my life was occupied with classes that were taught by the bishop himself. How lucky we were to have him for our teacher.

One unusual aspect of being the absolute last member of the class of 1979 was that I was ordained last. Absolutely last. We were in alphabetical order: Montoya, Ortega, Perez, Ramirez, Sanchez, Trevino, Zamora, and Quinlan. So, being the last one in line to be ordained, the bishop and his aide were right behind me. Bishop Leven had just had by-pass heart surgery and Bishop Rumundo Piña, who at the time was the Auxiliary Bishop of San Antonio, was the ordaining bishop. The bishop's aide was in conversation with my wife and the bishop and I are sizing each other up. He stood there with his miter and crosier and he said to me, "Are you nervous?" "Yes, Bishop," I said. "Not to worry," he said, "you've never done this before, I have."

Being a Full-Time Deacon

I have for a very long time felt very strongly that the best resource a pastor without an assistant at a large parish had was that of a full-time deacon. The deacon would be there on the priest's day off, would be there to handle routine sacramentals like blessing of religious articles, and would handle requests for financial assistance by walk-ins. The deacon would be available to answer questions over the phone regarding marriage, annulments and baptisms.

By virtue of his training and ordination the deacon possesses certain credibility in talking about church policy, rituals and rites. Anything he is not comfortable addressing he can refer or take down the question and get back to the person after doing some research.

Working in concert with the parish secretary, a person asking to see a priest is immediately asked the question, "Are you seeking absolution?" If the answer is "No. I need bus fare to Pueblo, Colorado," then the secretary simply says, "Please have a seat and the deacon will see you directly." Together, we have side-stepped another unnecessary waste of the priest's time because the deacon can determine the need as well as the priest. The priest could be spending his time doing priestly things, and the deacon becomes an extension, another set of hands.

Another area I think deserves consideration is that the deacon should have the faculty for administering the Sacrament of the Sick. I know there are a lot of priests that will argue the link with the Sacrament of the Sick and the Sacrament of Reconciliation, but in over 20 years of ordained Roman Catholic ministry I have never heard a dying person say, "I can't receive Viaticum because I need to go to Confession." Most of the people I watch priests anoint are heavily sedated, comatose, or are using machines to assist in breathing and could not confess anyway. As the situation gets worse with the shortage of priests, maybe the church will consider this option.

Job Interview

Though I actually did not place such an ad, below is what I could very well have stated when I was looking for a parish in the Denver area to serve in as a pastoral assistant:

> Experienced, full-time permanent deacon looking for a position in the Denver area. Ordained 20 years, 12 years in full-time ministry. BA and MA from UNC in Greeley. A 1987 graduate of St. Thomas Seminary. He is certified in Pastoral Care and has experience in Baptismal and Marriage Prep, Parish Advocate in Annulments. Is experienced in Outreach and Home visitations of Seniors, possesses good people skills. Has faculties to preach and enjoys hospital visitations. Regards himself as a priest's helper and a team player. A good man to have around on your day off.

I once applied for a position as a pastoral assistant at a large downtown Denver Catholic Church. I was asked to come by for an interview by the pastor. I arrived at the rectory on time and thought the interview went quite well. Father said I would be hearing from him in a week or so.

The following week I was asked to return for a second interview, but this time it would be at the Chancery and not at the rectory. The pastor had a position at the Chancery as well as being a pastor. His secretary asked me if I would like a Coke and I said yes. She returned a few minutes later with two Cokes in beautiful leaded glasses on a silver tray.

The pastor and I got into the second interview and everything was going fine. All of a sudden the conversation stalled, a bit embarrassing to say the least. I said to the pastor, "Is there anything I can say or do to convince you that I am the right man for the job?" He smiled at me and held up his leaded Coke glass and asked, "Can you turn this into bourbon?" Well, we both laughed. I said to myself, "Tom, you can work for this man. He has a genuine sense of humor."

I got the job and we had a great relationship as pastor and deacon for three years.

You Owe Me

During the summer of 1975 I was transferred from the Air Force Academy in Colorado Springs, Colorado to Dyess AFB, in Abilene Texas. The house in the Springs had not sold yet, so I left for Abilene by myself. When the house sold, I was to fly back for the closing and drive our second car with my wife and two sons to Abilene.

I was going to try to make the trip in one long day. By the time I got to Abilene, it was late at night and, although it was dark and I had been driving for 15 hours, I thought I could find the Air Base. Wrong. I could not. I drove around and around and just could not find it.

In total desperation I stopped at an all-night convenience store and asked a fellow putting gas in his motorcycle if he could give me directions to Dyess AFB. He simply smiled and said, "Sure. Come follow me," and off we went. As it turned out I was only a few miles from what is called the Texas Street Gate. When we got there and I got out of the car to thank the fellow, he said to me, "You owe me."

I reached for my billfold and he said, "No, I don't mean money. Sometime during your stay here in Abilene, someone is going to do the same thing that you did to me, and to pay me back you are to escort them to the closest gate. Understood?" "You bet," I said. With that he gave me his business card, turned around and started his motorcycle and was gone. The business card identified him as the pastor of the Abilene Church of the Four Square.

For the next four years that I lived in the town of Abilene and was assigned to Dyess AFB, I paid back this act of Christian charity time and time again. One day after work I was in the local discount store buying materials for a home project. I was in the checkout line and could see this young man, looking very tired, carrying a baby, his wife beside him with three other children.

He came up to me and said, "Excuse me Captain, I have been assigned to Dyess AFB, and I can't seem to find it. Can you help me please?" I smiled, picked up my supplies and said, "Come, follow me." I escorted him to the Main Gate, got out of my car to speak to him and said, "You owe me." I then explained the rules: He was to be available at any time to do the same thing that I had just done for him and his family.

It's nice to think that at this very moment in Abilene, Texas a person is being directed to the Air Base by a perfect stranger and will begin to carry out the tradition of helping one's neighbor in simple Christian charity with the words of our Savior, Jesus Christ, who said, "Come, Follow Me."

As a sad addendum to this story, during my time in Abilene I heard that the young pastor of the Church of the Four Square was killed. A driver ran a red light and broadsided his motorcycle. He was killed instantly.

Archbishop

I first met the new archbishop of Denver, Colorado, Most Rev. Charles Chaput, O.F.M., Cap. in the summer of 1987. I had just graduated from St. Thomas Seminary and my first full-time job as a Pastoral Assistant was at St. Elizabeth's Church on the Auraria Campus. I had an office just across the hall from him and we would see each other daily. At the time, he was the Provincial of the Mid-West Province of the Capuchin Friars.

While at St. Elizabeth's I also attended the Westland Nursing Home in Lakewood. I received a call that one of the Catholic residents was dying and needed the Sacrament of the Sick and Viaticum. Fr. Charles was in, so I asked him if he could accompany me to anoint a dying resident and I would administer the Viaticum. He said he would be happy to accompany me.

On the drive out we got the chance to learn a little more about each other. I told him about living in Conifer with my wife and two sons, and he shared with me about his Native American heritage and priesthood in the Capuchin Order. He was very easy to talk to.

When we arrived at Westland, he was warm and friendly to all the staff. He anointed the dying resident and as I gave the Blessed Sacrament he held the person's hand. I could see in the face of the dying resident that Fr. Charles had an unusual ability to make a person who was afraid of dying feel at peace. When we left, I knew I had been privileged to be part of a very special sacramental experience.

I Knew a Saint

I was privileged during my third and fourth year of full time ministry as a Pastoral Assistant/Deacon to meet and become friends with a woman whom I believe was a saint in her lifetime. I met her at a nursing home that was geographically in the parish. We would have Mass there every Wednesday and all the Catholic residents would attend. Every three months a priest would anoint all the Catholic residents. That way there would be no need for Father to come by at 2 a.m. when a resident was near death.

This lady whom I think was a saint had a unique quality about her. She was very comfortable with the issue of death and would sit up half the night with a resident who was dying to "help him cross over," as she called it. She would do this on a regular basis, spending untold hours with dying patients. The floor nurses loved her because when she was there they could be attending to some other duty. This ease she had with the dying was well known throughout the nursing home.

I often asked her to offer her services to the faculty at St. Thomas Seminary. There were many young men I knew who were studying for the priesthood who could benefit from spending some time with her, listening to her, and watching her interact with the dying. There was something very spiritual about her. She was quiet and had eyes that seemed to see right through you. There was always a quiet air of connectedness with the patient, and you got the feeling that she was in direct communication with God.

The day that I found out she had terminal cancer I was shocked beyond belief. I called her and we talked. Several weeks later I ran into her at the nursing home and she said she had a present for me. She wanted me to have her pyx (the special container for the Eucharist). As the end grew closer, I saw less and less of her until she called me and asked me to come by her place so she could say goodbye in a proper fashion.

I arrived at her condo and she was waiting for me in the foyer, wearing a robe and looking very pale and drawn. She said she wanted to say goodbye to me before she had to start taking heavy drugs to kill the pain. We chatted for awhile and I told her I would really like her blessing. I got up off the divan and knelt in front of her. She put her hands on my head and gave me her blessing. The last thing she said to me really took me by surprise. She said to ask in prayer for her to intercede in my behalf if I ever needed anything.

I know she was never canonized a saint in the Roman Catholic Church, but I have this gut level feeling that she was a saint while on earth and she is a saint in heaven.

Announcing the
Banns of Marriage

I had the pleasure of preparing a very unusual couple
for marriage. The couple was unusual in that the groom
was an Israeli Christian. He showed me his Israeli pass-
port which stated that he was a Christian and had special provisions that waived restrictions that Jewish
Israelis had to comply with.

The marriage preparation was routine but the conse-
quences following the marriage prep were very unusual. The wedding was to take place in Israel in a church
that the groom's father helped build near Bethlehem.
The local bishop would perform the wedding.

One morning the phone rang and it was a Monsignor
from Bethlehem. He said he was the aide for the bishop and wanted me to fax him a certificate stating that
the banns of marriage had been announced three times.
I tried to explain to him that we stopped announcing
the banns of marriage after Vatican II, but he insisted
that it be done. He gave me his fax number and told me
he wanted the certificate in two hours.

Every once in awhile I think you need to be flexible
and bend a little. So I went over to the church, turned
on the PA system and announced the banns of marriage
three times from the pulpit. Then I typed a letter on
church stationery, put the parish seal on it, and ran it
across the street to a convenience store with a fax ser-

vice. In less than three minutes I sent the letter and confirmed its delivery.

The first Christmas of their marriage the new bride stopped by the Sacristy after mass and presented me with a small wooden camel made from olive wood from Israel. I keep the gift on my desk as a reminder to be flexible and bend a little.

(Author's note: In my defense against the argument that this story makes light of canon law, let me say that the episcopal conferences world-wide have not progressed at the same speed, and in some places in the world there is still a requirement to read the banns of marriage three times. I mean no disrespect to canon law. I simply tried to comply with a direct order from the aide to the bishop.)

Still in Charge

I once had the distinct privilege of ministering to a wonderful Methodist lady. I met her at a nursing home where I was attending the lady in the next bed. I had several brief conversations with her before the lady I was attending died. Later, I came by to say hello and we soon developed a very nice friendship. As sick as she was, she always seemed to be in charge.

She became very ill and was transferred to the hospital. It was while she was in the hospital that she asked me to officiate at her funeral. I asked her if it might be more appropriate for a Methodist minister to do that and she said that in all the time she had been sick I was the only minister that came to see her. I agreed, and she picked out the scripture readings and the music. She said there was only one thing about me that irritated her, and that was that when any of the other ladies had their minister come see them, their minister LOOKED like a minister, I always seemed to look like I was going jogging.

When the end grew near, she was transferred to a Hospice nearby and I visited her regularly. I mentioned to her that I did not like the artificial flowers next to her bed and asked her if it would be okay if I bought her a plant. She said yes, she would like that. I went to the florist and picked out a nice plant, but I had no idea what to put on the card. I finally wrote, "Dear Viola, I'm going to loan you this plant, and when you are finished with it, I would like it back. That way I will have something to remember you by. Love, Deacon Tom."

One evening I came by to see her and the bed was gone. I was stunned. I knew it would happen but I was not prepared for it that day. I started to walk out past the nurses station, which was quite busy, when I saw a nurse with a phone to her ear looking at me and snapping her fingers to get my attention. She ended her conversation and put the phone down and said, "Are you the Catholic deacon from Conifer that comes here to see Viola?" "Yes," I said. She reached under the desk and pulled out the plant and said, "Viola left this for you."

I put the plant in the back seat of the car and covered it with an old field jacket to keep it warm as the day was very cold. When I got home I felt under the leaves to see if the plant needed to be watered and my hand felt a card. The card was from Viola. It said, "Dear Deacon Tom, I am finished with your plant, you can have it back now. I love you very much, Viola."

I did the funeral in the chapel at the cemetery. There were a lot of people there and I could see the confused look on many of the faces when I introduced myself as a Catholic deacon. I explained that Viola did not convert to Catholicism before she died. She was very comfortable being a Methodist and I was comfortable with her being a Methodist. Then I explained how I had come to know Viola.

Several months went by when one evening I received a phone call from a Denver attorney. He asked me if I had attended Viola and I said yes. He said that Viola had mentioned me in her will and he wanted to talk to me personally and read an excerpt from the will. It read, "To Deacon Tom Quinlan, the Catholic deacon from Conifer, I bequeath the sum of one hundred and fifty dollars for him to purchase proper clergy garb so he may represent the Roman Church more fully."

God Bless Viola, still in charge even after death.

Pulling the Plug

One of the most unusual hospital visits I ever made was at the request of my pastor. He called me on the intercom at the church office and asked if I could take the Blessed Sacrament to National Jewish Hospital to a patient and to be in the Intensive Care Unit at exactly 12 noon. I said yes and arranged my morning accordingly.

At exactly 12 noon I walked into the ICU looking for the patient. A young woman came toward me dressed in a business suit and asked me if I was the deacon. I said yes. She introduced herself as the daughter of the man I was there to see. She informed me that her father was a very important public relations executive for a large corporation and that I was not there to give communion.

Her father, she explained, had come from Las Vegas 58 days before and had gone into a coma two days later. He had not regained consciousness and they were going to unplug all life support systems. I was there to hold his hand while he died.

I could not believe what I was hearing. Hold his hand while he died! How could an ordinary hospital visit get so screwed up. Emotionally, I was not prepared for this. I was simply there to give communion, not this.

Next thing I knew, I was holding his hand as they were unplugging him from the life support. Everybody was watching him except me. My eyes were closed and

I was praying for all I was worth. Nearly 40 minutes later he was declared dead and I was an emotional wreck.

The daughter was busy with a cell phone making arrangements with the pilot of their private jet to transport the body back home to Las Vegas. No one said goodbye to me. No one said thank you. I didn't say anything either. I just sort of floated out of there in a fog. I stopped by the office and told the secretary that I would not be coming back to work that day. If there was an emergency, I could be reached at home. I drove slowly, methodically, thinking about what had happened. When I got home I took a nap and then went for a long walk.

Most things in my life happen for a reason. What was the reason for this? Was there a lesson to be learned? Maybe, maybe not. That day was a test of my preparedness to minister and I just barely passed. I thank God for the strength he gave me to stay there and hold the man's hand and pray. I really wanted to run out and leave the whole crazy scene.

From then on I would not take going to a hospital as routine. I will never forget what happened to me and would be on my guard to be prepared for the unexpected.

Pentecost at Dutch Harbor

In the early nineties I was invited to spend a week in Dutch Harbor, Alaska to help commemorate the 50th Anniversary of the bombing of the island by the Japanese. When I got to the island, which is out in the Aleutian Chain off the coast of Alaska, I was beginning to feel a little like James Bond. I would be the official Amateur (HAM) Radio Station for the event. A facility would be available for my use.

I also was invited to function as a deacon when it became known that I was going to be on the island over Pentecost. Temporary faculties were granted and a nun would meet my plane at the Anchorage airport with a ciborium of consecrated hosts. If I had not been there, the bishop would have sent a priest. The airfare would have cost over a thousand dollars.

The Communion Service outside the Mass with Homily was a success. The Catholic residents and the fishermen, mainly Mexican and Portuguese, were very happy to attend a Catholic service on this holy day.

The HAM radio part of my trip also was very successful. The island was highly sought after by HAMS from all over the world and I made over 5,000 contacts.

The icing on the cake was that many of the Catholic residents came to see me off at the airport and presented me with a large container of frozen crab. The airport manager waived all excess baggage fees and the crab was still frozen when it arrived in Denver.

Attending the Needs
of a Family in Crisis

The phone woke me at one o'clock in the morning. The caller, my tax man, was also on the local Volunteer Fire Department. He knew that I was a Catholic deacon and called me because he was at the site of a suicide and the family was Catholic.

I asked to speak to a family member and was connected to the mother. I explained to her that I would be available to arrive on scene to bless the body but not to administer the Sacrament of the Sick, or "the Last Rites" as some people still call it. I wanted her to clearly understand just what I would be doing so there would be no confusion. She said she understood. I assured her I would leave directly, got good directions from the fireman and started on my way.

When I arrived at the house, the place was crowded with vehicles with flashing lights. I was cleared into the restricted area, given a badge and escorted to an area where the family had gathered.

The young man who had committed suicide was in his mid-twenties and had recently been accused of a sexual crime involving young Boy Scouts. He had closed himself up in the family garage with a Jeep Cherokee, connected a hose from the exhaust to the inside of the vehicle, got in, and turned on the engine. He died of carbon monoxide poisoning.

After talking with the family for a while, the mom and I went to the garage where the son was in a black body bag on a gurney. A fireman unzipped the bag halfway down so we were able to get a good look at him.

The mom and I prayed the Lord's Prayer. I then said an impromptu prayer asking God to be merciful to a young man who was overcome with grief and despair and ended with the Animi Christi, "Out of the depths I have cried to you, O Lord," etc. I blessed him with the Sign of the Cross with Holy Water.

We returned to the family and I drank a cup of coffee with them. I gave the mother my business card to give to the local priest. When funeral arrangements were made I wanted her to explain that I simply blessed the body and did not anoint him.

I mention this incident because all too often, if not explained, what I did is misinterpreted as a deacon administrating the Sacrament of the Sick.

Wedding in Breckenridge

There was a local couple from our parish preparing to get married in an ecumenical service at the Father Dyer Memorial Chapel in Breckenridge. One of the interesting things about this chapel is that Father Dyer was a Methodist minister who everybody called Father. The story goes that Father Dyer used to carry the mail from Alma to Leadville in the winter on foot during the gold rush days in Colorado. He had a church there and most of his congregation were Irish and German prospectors who were Catholic. He picked up the title of Father because that's all his congregation knew to call their clergy.

At the time of this wedding, the pastor of the chapel was a very nice woman who had talked to me several times over the phone about my involvement in the wedding. The groom was Catholic and the bride was Methodist. The mother of the groom wanted a Catholic presence and was having a problem getting the local priest to be that presence because the wedding time conflicted with the Saturday evening mass of anticipation. The mother told me that if I would assist at the wedding and bring my wife along, she would put us up at the Breckenridge Hilton for the night. My wife thought this would be a good way for us to get away for a nice weekend.

Now to get to the story. A half hour before the wedding, the groom, his best man and about four others, all part of the groom's party, asked the pastor if they could use her office in private for a little male bonding. A little strange I thought, but the pastor said okay, and we left them alone.

The wedding started on time and at its completion the pastor and I went back into her office to remove our vestments. There we discovered an empty six-pack of beer and an empty bottle of peppermint schnapps. The introduction of liquor at a religious ceremony in both Catholic and Methodist weddings could invalidate the marriage if the groom were found to be under the influence of alcohol. The pastor agreed with me that we needed to get the groom and his party back in there to find out what was going on.

When all were assembled we addressed the issue and they all were a little embarrassed. The pastor and I expressed our disappointment at such juvenile behavior and wanted to know who had done the drinking. All of the groom's party admitted drinking the beer and the schnapps, with the exception of the groom. Much to our delight, the groom stated that he had not taken a drink, just his best man and the groomsmen. I was satisfied, as was the Methodist pastor, and so we dismissed them and headed for the reception.

The reason I even share this story with you is that if the groom had been drinking it could have been cause to tell the bride, groom and the wedding party that they would have to come back the next day because the ceremony was not valid. If in a few years the bride and groom divorced and the Catholic party attempted to receive an annulment on the grounds that he was drunk during the ceremony and could prove that the male bonding ceremony consisted of drinking a bottle of schnapps and a six-pack of beer, a marriage tribunal could be influenced into determining that the marriage was invalid from the start.

Baptism at Night

A local parish family asked me if I would be agreeable to doing a baptism at night. A weekend night seemed to be the only time they could get the godparents together because of work conflicts and shift schedules.

I met the family at 7:00 p.m. on a very cold and dark night for the baptism. I unlocked the church and as we entered the baptistery I turned on the single light in the ceiling. It lit and popped and everything was black. I needed at least enough light so we could read "The Rite of Baptism" booklet.

The only thing I could think to use was altar candles. There were about a dozen people there so I asked half of them to follow me up to the main altar to bring back candles to use in the baptistery. We lit the candles and it really looked bright and warm in the baptistery. I could read and they could follow along. It was a very special baptism.

When we were finished we carried the candles back to the main altar. As we got to the front of the church there was a child, a little girl about six or so, doing a little ballet dance. It was quite nice and most of us stopped to watch. All of a sudden the little girl's father walked up with his candle and in a loud voice of disapproval said, "Mary Beth, what do you think you are doing?"

The youngster stopped in her tracks, frightened at

her fathers' disapproval, and a hush fell over the group. With childhood innocence she responded, "I'm dancing for God."

The response took my breath away as well as that of most of the people there. We had come that night to witness a sacrament and at the very conclusion were part of one.

The Real Presence

I was born in the late thirties and was a youngster during World War II while my father was in the Pacific Theater fighting the Japanese. I must have been more than my mom could handle because I wound up in a military academy in Oakland, New Jersey at the age of six.

One of the rules at Oakland Military Academy was that you had to attend church. My mom must have filled the form out incorrectly because the school claimed that the church affiliation block was left blank. This gave the school the option to send me to a different church each week. One of the commandant's favorite expressions was "All my young men go to church." Consequently, at age six I had a variety of experiences in going to Methodist, Episcopal, Reformed, Baptist, as well as Roman Catholic churches.

Our Lady of the Assumption, a Catholic Church attended by the Franciscan Fathers (O.F.M.), was in Pompton Lakes, New Jersey, the town next to Oakland. This was where I went when it came my turn to go to the Catholic Church. As young as I was, I felt there was something different about the Catholic Church. I really got the feeling of the presence of God in that church. It was an experience I have never forgotten and always cherish in my heart.

Many years later, early in 1970, I returned from a two-year assignment in Turkey. I was on my way to Da

Nang Air Base, Republic of Viet Nam. My wife and son needed a place to live and we chose New Jersey to be close to my parents. We worked with realtors with no success. Finally, I put an ad in several local newspapers and got a response from a lady who heard of my situation. We went to see the house, signed the lease and made arrangements to have the household goods delivered, gas and electric turned on, and a phone installed.

The great part of this story was that the house, in case you have not already guessed, was in Pompton Lakes and the nearest Catholic Church was Our Lady of the Assumption. Coincidence or divine intervention?

Nothing by Mouth

Those of you doing hospital ministry will probably see "NBM" displayed at the head of the bed or somewhere prominent. It means that the patient cannot receive anything by mouth, including the Blessed Sacrament in host form.

I have two small brown bottles with eye dropper cap tops in my hospital kit. One bottle contains sterile water and the other consecrated wine. The bottles are scotch-taped together and the contents labeled. If I enter a hospital room and see the NBM notation for a patient who desires to receive the Blessed Sacrament, I go to the nurses station and ask to talk to the patient's nurse. I show her the glass containers and explain the contents and that one drop of the consecrated wine is the same as a host. Usually I get a nod of approval, sometimes not.

If I get permission, I administer the consecrated wine as I would the host with the proper prayers. After giving the patient the consecrated wine, I put the eye dropper top cap into the sterile water so as not to contaminate the consecrated wine. The bottle is then ready to be used again. When I get home I can sterilize the used eye dropper cap top.

My view is that I have made an overture to allow a patient the option of receiving the Blessed Sacrament. I have a strong belief in the healing power of the Blessed Sacrament. During the times I was in the hospital I was happy to receive the Blessed Sacrament before my surgery. It just made me feel a lot better.

Funerals

It seems that in every parish I have been assigned to the pastor likes me to do the cemetery part of the funeral. That's okay because I like getting out of the office. But the two cemeteries in the local area, Fort Logan and Mount Olivet, have got to be the coldest places in the county in the wintertime.

I remember one time I was asked to do the committal. We drove in procession from the church to the cemetery, picked up the escort from the cemetery at the front gate, and were led to the grave site where chairs were set up for friends and family. The pall bearers carried the coffin to the grave site.

I was just getting ready to begin when the escort from the cemetery came driving up, horn blaring. She got out of the escort vehicle and yelled at the top of her voice, "Wrong grave. Wrong grave." Well, the cemetery representative was embarrassed, the funeral director was embarrassed, the family was angry and I thought it was hilariously funny.

When we got to the right grave, I could sense everyone was ill at ease. So I said, "I knew Hazel quite well. I visited her at home often and brought her the Blessed Sacrament. Hazel had a wonderful sense of humor, and I'll just bet she is looking down from heaven and having a good laugh." That got many smiles and a chuckle or two and put everyone at ease so we could continue.

Holy Communion

In all the years I have been ordained I still get a feeling of awe when I think about distributing the Blessed Sacrament. One occasion, however, almost became funny.

Here in Colorado there is not a lot of humidity and there is a lot of static electricity which occasionally affects communion hosts. One Sunday I was distributing Holy Communion and was having a problem with the hosts sticking together. It was like they were magnetized and it slowed me down quite a bit. All of a sudden this young man appeared before me as I was trying to break loose a host. I glanced up at him and then at the ciborium and tried to pick up just one host. The young man said to me, "Any one will do."

(Author's note: Before you turn the page, I need to say something to the reader. This deacon has a very strong faith in the Real Presence of the Blessed Sacrament and I share this story with you so you may experience the human aspect of ministry in the real world. People say things that under any other circumstances would be mundane; here there was an honest misinterpretation of what I was doing, not picking out a special host but simply trying to break one loose from those that were electrostatically charged. In all sincereity, I mean no disrespect.)

Expect the Unexpected

Art Linkletter used to say that "Kids say the darndest things." I feel the same way about senior citizens.

One of the Eucharistic Ministers was going on vacation and asked me if I could take Communion to an elderly parishioner until she got back. I was able to fit it into my schedule and at the appointed day and time arrived at the house. After she let me in and was seated, I began. We prayed together and I gave her the Blessed Sacrament.

When I finished, she said that she was a cradle Catholic, had buried two husbands and one son and only had one question for me. I asked what that would be. She said, "What the hell is a deacon?"

Hospital Kit

Ever since I was first ordained I have realized the need for a special hospital and nursing home kit for deacons – something that could fit into a sports jacket pocket and would contain a pyx for communion, the oils for baptism as well as the oils for administering the Sacrament of the Sick, and a book that would contain all of the proper prayers and rubrics for administering the sacraments. I also try to have a few medals of the Blessed Mother with the Memorare in a plastic envelope, as well as a few pairs of inexpensive rosaries to give away.

The reason I have included the Sacrament of the Sick is not because I ever intend on administering the sacrament, but having the oils and stole as well as the right prayers puts me in a pretty powerful bargaining position if I should find a Catholic priest walking the halls of a hospital where I need a patient anointed right away. It has happened that I have found a priest who was willing to administer the Sacrament of the Sick and used my kit.

When I was in formation to be a deacon I remember a priest told me that when you walk into a nursing home or hospital, you are, repeat, are, the Roman Catholic Church.

Proclamation Affirmation

I have been a deacon for 20 years and I think I have heard every possible response imaginable when folks come up for Communion. I have heard "Thank you," "So be it," "I believe," and the standard appropriate response "Amen." I make the proclamation and the recipient makes the affirmation. When I hear a new one it surprises me almost to the point where I come close to losing it.

Such an event occurred in my life on Sunday in January in Denver, which is the home of the National Western Stock Show. I had been assisting the pastor in the distribution of Holy Communion when I saw an older man walking down the center aisle to receive Communion. He was clean shaven and immaculately dressed in a tailored western suit. His boots had silver tips and he was wearing a large silver belt buckle. He was holding a beautiful gray Stetson western hat. As he approached me I held up a host and said, "The Body of Christ," to which he responded in a rich deep bass voice, "You bet."

Being Called Father

As a deacon, you are going to be called "Father." Don't let it bother you. There are two things you can do. One is to do nothing. Another is to correct immediately.

While visiting a priest friend in Trinidad, Colorado, I assisted him as deacon of the Mass. After Mass, we both stood at the bottom of the church steps and greeted the parishioners as they came out. It was a predominately Hispanic group and they all called me Father. My priest friend saw what was happening and called out to me, "Don't waste your breath. Just tell them they have a beautiful church and you are enjoying yourself here in Trinidad."

I went into the Sacristy to take off my vestments and there was a long line of people silently waiting. I asked them if I could be of any help and they told me they were waiting to buy seven-day votive candles. In the next two and a half minutes I did over $150 worth of candle business. Father told me the candle sales allowed him to continue an outreach ministry to feed the hungry.

Football

At the church where I was assigned we often got the service of order priests to help out on the weekends since we had one priest and 2,600 registered families.

One weekend the visiting priest, an avid football fan, was sitting in the priest's chair with the deacon beside him. For some reason he started to stand up, got about half way, and then sat down when he realized he was not supposed to be standing. Well, when he started to stand, the congregation also started to stand and then sit down again. After everyone was seated the priest leaned over and whispered to the deacon, "I made them jump offside."

Being Part of the Family

In late January I received a call from the answering service at the church. They had received a call regarding a death and asked me to please respond to it since the pastor was out of town. The call was from registered parishioners who had experienced the death of the grandfather of the family. The deceased had died out of state and the family wanted the deacon to come to the house and do a Memorial Communion Service outside the Mass with homily on Sunday evening at 7:00 p.m.

I arrived at 6:40 p.m. I recognized the address as I had been there the previous summer to bless the house. It was all starting to come back to me. The family was from India and were strong Catholics.

When I entered the house there must have been 30 adults present and at least a dozen children. All the adult women were wearing saris, beautiful jewelry, and a jewel in their pierced noses. All were dark skinned with dark hair. The men were all wearing suits and ties. In contrast, the teenagers had on Reboks, jeans, and Bronco football jackets.

I was shown to a bedroom where I could vest. There I had a chance to inquire about the grandfather's age, cause of death, occupation, etc. The man of the house came in and asked me if it would be all right for the assembled group to sing appropriate church songs in their native language. Naturally I said yes.

I set up for a Communion Service on a low table. Everyone was seated on the floor. The wall to wall carpet was covered with oriental rugs throughout the house. Music was provided by one of the seated men with a keyboard type organ about 12-by-24-by-15 inches deep. The musician played the organ with his right hand and opened and closed a baffle at the rear of the organ to provide the forced air necessary to make music. The tunes all had an eastern flair and were sung with great enthusiasm. They sang one song at the beginning, another after the Gospel, and a third after Communion.

Thirty people received Communion. They knew the responses by heart, that is to say they all recited the Glory to God, the Profession of Faith, The Lord's Prayer, and at Communion they all made a fist and struck their breast at the Lamb of God. When I finished, a friend of the deceased gave a moving eulogy that was translated into English by one of the sons.

As I walked back to the bedroom to take off my vestments, I got a chill up my spine as the thought occurred to me that this is what church is all about. I had been present and presided over a very special religious event that night and I was truly blessed.

Expecting a Miracle

Just when you think you have all your ducks in a row, the human aspect of your ministry plays a part and throws you a curve you were not expecting. Let me cite you an example.

Another deacon and myself were attending a local family, an older couple both in their sixties. The mom had terminal cancer. The other deacon attended the mom and I attended the dad. We spent many an hour talking about what was going to happen – the eventual death of the mom. We walked together along the five step road of acceptance according to Dr. Elizabeth Kubler-Ross' book on death and dying. I was pretty sure the dad was in the acceptance stage, or so I thought. Wrong!

The other deacon and I used to car pool to their home. One evening when we arrived the house was dark and no one was at home. We drove away confused and returned several days later to the same dark, empty house. We knew there were family members in Denver, but they were all married girls. We had no idea of their married names, so we just waited.

Four or five days later I received a phone call from one of the daughters. She was sorry no one had thought to call the deacons until then, but she wanted to explain just what had happened. She told me her dad, in a state of desperation, withdrew $60,000 from the bank, bought a motor home, and drove his wife to Mexico for laetrile treatments. Laetrile is not a drug approved by the U.S. government, so folks seeking treatment went across the border into Mexico where clinics offered it.

The mom had died the second day she was there. The Mexican government would not allow the dad to take the body out of the country. He just wanted to bring her home to Colorado, but the Mexican government said no. The only way they would let him out of the country is if he had the mom cremated. He then could bring the cremains back in a vase.

By this point, the dad was a wreck. He crossed the border and drove to his married daughter's house in California. After several days he realized that he was unable to drive the motor home to Colorado. He flew back and his son-in-law drove the motor home to Colorado. There was a Mass at the local Catholic Church and the cremains were interred in the local cemetery.

The other deacon and I scratched our heads asking each other what did we do wrong. After a lot of soul searching and introspection, we both admitted to gross errors in not realizing the extent of the husband's emotional condition. We thought he was in the acceptance stage when in fact he was still in the denial stage. When the smoke cleared, both the other deacon and I received a very nice card from the dad thanking us for our efforts and explaining to us "the rest of the story."

Moral: When you think you have everything going along really smooth and the person you are ministering to is acting in a predictable way, be prepared for a curve – something off the wall like a spur of the moment flight to Mexico.

Conditional Baptism

A young couple in our parish was expecting a baby. The husband called me from the hospital and said that the baby had been born dead. He asked me to please come by the hospital as soon as possible to be there for the family.

When I arrived at the hospital I talked with the husband in the hall outside of the wife's room in order to size up the situation. I had brought the Blessed Sacrament with me and explained to the couple that I personally felt it had marvelous healing power. I asked them if they wanted to receive it and they both said yes. After the rite was completed, the wife threw me a curve by asking if I would baptize the baby. I explained the gray areas of conditional baptism and agreed to do it.

They explained what they wanted to the nurse assigned to handle all the needs of a mom who loses a baby. The nurse brought the baby from the morgue to a room next to the mom's room. The baby was presented in a new fresh blanket. It was bruised about the face and neck, but was beautiful. The baby had lots of hair. I would guess it was about seven pounds. It was very still and cold. The nurse had laid out a stainless steel miniature pitcher and there was a baptismal certificate for me to fill out and present to the family.

The dad and I were left alone with the baby. I baptized the baby and the father and I prayed over his dead son. It was a terribly sad scene and at the same time it reaffirmed our common belief in life after death. When we finished, the nurse came in and removed the baby's body.

The dad and I rejoined the mom in her room. She broke down and told us that she wanted to be there. I sat next to her and told her I thought that would have been a bad idea. I told her I wanted her to remember her baby as she remembered him at delivery. He was bruised and, because he was dead, the bruises would not go away. I did not want her to see him in that condition. When I learned there was a sibling at home, I suggested to the mom and dad that when they try to explain what had happened they should stress that the sibling now had a brother in heaven and that the brother had a name.

Part of the unexplainable aspect of this case lies in the fact that up until a few hours before the delivery, everything seemed to be okay. An autopsy was performed to determine the exact cause of death. Results indicated that the baby had a spasm and a bowel movement had contaminated the area. The baby was poisoned by its own fluids.

Since no one knows at what point the soul leaves the body at death, it is strictly a judgment call as to when a conditional baptism is appropriate or not. In this case I felt that it would aid in closure for the family. I knew that a child that was alive such a short time had no opportunity to sin, and when his soul left the body it went straight to heaven. If I was wrong and I violated a rule or the law of God, I was prepared to pay the price because I believed what I did was proper under the circumstances.

Food for the Journey

Recently, my pastor asked me to visit a dying patient in a local hospital and take him Viaticum. I knew that I would find a sign over the bed that said NBM, nothing by mouth, so I called and talked to his nurse before leaving. You can give a patient Viaticum in the form of consecrated wine without breaking the NBM rule of the hospital.

I have two small medicine bottles taped together and labeled. Both bottles have eye dropper tops. One bottle contains the most precious blood (consecrated wine) and the other has sterile water. After putting a drop or so in the mouth of the patient, you put the top from the sterile water on the consecrated wine and the top that you just put in the mouth of the patient is placed in the sterile water. That way you can clean the used top in a diluted bleach solution when you return to the church. To not contaminate one patient with bodily fluid from another, you never administer Viaticum to more than one patient in this way.

I met with the family in the hospital hallway and told them of my plan to administer Viaticum in the form of consecrated wine. I explained to the family the theory that the dying and those in a coma sometimes may hear everything that goes on in the room. I asked the family if anybody had given the father "permission" to go. I explained that many older people hang on and on because they feel guilty in leaving and that family members need to say, "It's all right."

We all went into the hospital room and prayed together. Then one of the daughters removed the oxygen mask briefly as the other daughter said, "Daddy, the deacon is here with food for your journey." I said, "The Blood of Christ," and put a drop or two in his mouth and replaced the oxygen mask. I looked around and there were tears and smiles on everyone's face. The family thanked me for coming by and bringing their dad the spiritual food for his journey to be with our Heavenly Father.

The Holy Spirit at Work

A parishioner called and asked if I would baptize her dad, Ray, who was in his late seventies and had incurable cancer. I told her I would really like to meet her dad and have a talk with him.

We arranged a meeting and I was very impressed with Ray. Although wheelchair-bound, he was quite mobile. He told me he was a life-long Methodist, but never baptized. He had been married to a Catholic for almost 40 years and his wife had died several years ago. She was a strong Catholic and had raised their only child in the faith. Ray said he always felt that having one Catholic in the family was enough. Now that his wife was gone, he thought he needed to be that Catholic presence.

We had a nice talk about the Catholic Church and our beliefs. I was impressed with his knowledge of the faith and of Mary and the saints. We talked about baptism and Eucharist. I forgot that the man was married to a Catholic for almost 40 years and a lot of it must have rubbed off.

The family arranged for a private baptism on a weekday afternoon. About 30 relatives and friends showed up. It was a good crowd. When it came time for the baptism, Ray insisted that he stand up and, with assistance, walked to the front and was baptized. When it came time for him to receive his First Holy Communion, there were tears in his eyes, as well as all those assembled, including myself. When it was finished everybody clapped. I presented Ray with two certificates signed by the pastor certifying to his baptism and First Holy Communion.

Ray died about six months later. His daughter called and made arrangements for a Funeral Mass. She specifically asked that I lead the rosary at the funeral home. It was one of the most up-beat rosaries I have ever done. Everybody was in good spirits because Ray had made the journey to where we all hope to be someday. He led a good life, had a great marriage, a wonderful daughter, and toward the end made a religious conversion to become a member of the Catholic Church.

What I saw was the Holy Spirit at work in the world. Ray was an example for all of us. His personal spiritual journey, his cancer, his sincere belief that this was the right thing to do and doing it was something to behold. His daughter told me that toward the end he became a truly faith-filled person and was at peace.

Ray, if you hear my words, you were an inspiration. Whenever I get beat down and my faith starts to falter, I think of you. Thanks.

The Hitchhiker

I hardly ever pick up hitchhikers, but that day was different. I was on my way home from a day of teaching in Denver and I saw this young man by the side of the highway. He was standing next to a duffle bag which told me "U.S. Army." He had short hair and clean shaven which also told me "U.S. Army." So, I pulled over and stopped.

I was right. He had just mustered out of Ft. Carson, south of Colorado Springs, and was hitchhiking back home. We talked along the route about his service experiences. He liked Colorado, but needed to get home to get his civilian life going again, a job and his girlfriend, in that order.

As we drove through Aspen Park and Conifer I showed him where the new Catholic Church was being built. I told him I was the Catholic deacon for the new Our Lady of the Pines, and told him I would drop him at a spot I thought was the best possible place to get another ride.

I kind of felt that he did not have a lot of money, so when I stopped to let him out I pulled out my wallet to give him my business card and a five-dollar bill. To my surprise, the only bill I had in my wallet was a brand new twenty-dollar bill that my wife had given to me that morning. It was my lunch money for the next week. What was I going to do? From my perspective, the only thing I could do was to give him the twenty.

He certainly needed it more than me. He was shocked but very appreciative. He told me he had less than $50 cash as he had sent his Army pay home in money orders. We shook hands, he shut the door and waved goodbye.

End of story, not by a long shot. Several months later I received a letter with a note attached from the postmaster in Conifer. The little note said that after some thought she figured out who the letter was intended for. The letter simply said "To the Catholic Deacon, in Conifer Colorado 80433." It was from that young ex-Army hitchhiker. The letter said he thought I must have been good luck for him as it only took three rides past Conifer to get him back home. He said things were going great. His old boss rehired him with a nice raise, he bought a new car, and he and his girlfriend were engaged.

Lastly, inside the letter, wrapped in tissue, were six crisp twenty-dollar bills. One for me to replace the one I had given him, and $100 for the Building Fund at Our Lady of the Pines. Talk about bread upon the water. I never expected anything back, and look how it turned out.

No Guarantee

In the early eighties I met a local family in Conifer, Colorado. They were a Catholic family with eight children. The father worked in heavy equipment and did side jobs to help support his large family. The family and I became good friends.

The dad was not in good health. He had several hip replacements and walked with a limp and often used a cane. The dad got very sick and was hospitalized. I visited him and brought him the Blessed Sacrament every chance I could. I made sure he was anointed and was saddened when he died. I was the deacon of the Mass of the Resurrection.

After his burial, I got in my car with my wife. Rather than go directly home, I went to a hot tub store and put down a deposit. My wife, Glenys, had no idea what I was doing, so I explained that we had a list of things we wanted on the refrigerator door and one of the things we wanted was a hot tub, but the hot tub never moved up on the priority list. It just stayed where it was.

I explained to Glenys that if I had learned anything from my friend's death, it was simply that there was no guarantee for tomorrow. My friend worked hard all of his life trying to make ends meet for his family, and never enjoyed life. He would say that his enjoyable years would be when he retired. Well, he never got a chance to retire. He got sick and died.

So, what have I learned from all this? Quite simply

that in life there are no guarantees. If you want something that could bring you pleasure or happiness, you better get it and enjoy it now, because there is no guarantee you are going to live well into retirement.

We use the hot tub a lot, especially in the winter. It's therapeutic, it's relaxing, and it's the best natural sleeping pill you can take. Every time I slide into the tub, I think of my friend and say a small prayer for him. I named it the "Jim Halpin Memorial Hot Tub."

Being Left-Handed

The story I want to share with you is about being at a Denver, Colorado parish when the archbishop granted permission for us to have one Mass on Sunday, a Tridentine Mass, not quite an old-fashioned Latin Mass. My pastor asked me if I knew how to distribute the Blessed Sacrament in the old form, and of course I said yes. I had been an altar boy since I was in fourth grade and heard the priest say the words that I had memorized unconsciously.

I will not bore you with the complete ritual. If you are really interested, ask a priest who was ordained in the '50s. What I will tell you is that it is hard work and when you are done distributing the Blessed Sacrament, you are flat out of spit. That's the only way I can explain it. The deacon wears a surplice over a cassock with collar. I had no problem with the occasion and the ritual. However, the next day the pastor asked me to drop by the rectory, which I did.

He explained that the phone in the rectory had been ringing all afternoon with parishioners asking the same question. I had given them the Blessed Sacrament using my left hand and they wondered if the Blessed Sacrament was invalid by my not using the right hand. Can you believe it? I was concerned with the saying of the Latin prayer correctly before each recipient received Holy Communion, and the lay people were concerned about which hand I had used. I have read over and over, and friends, I don't have a clue whether Jesus, the Son of God, was left-handed or right-handed. Does it matter?

I guess looking at the total picture, the really important point is that the deacon needs to know everything that is going on, not just his role but the significance of everything. Why didn't someone bother to tell me about the right hand policy and why we do things the way that we do? The ritual is just as important for the priest and congregation as it should be for the deacon.

A Funeral Homily

Having the faculty to preach is a great honor and I don't take it lightly. I think a funeral homily is the hardest and the most emotional. When I was first ordained I had only one funeral homily and I would just make small changes and it would work for all occasions. I thought I might be making a big mistake and should have a half-dozen homilies to pick and choose to fit the occasion.

Then I saw a movie that had a very strong effect on me, *"Saving Private Ryan,"* (© 1999 Dream Works LLC, and Paramount Pictures Corp.), with Tom Hanks. In the movie, a World War II Army captain is sent into the field after the Normandy invasion to find Private Ryan, the sole surviving son of the Ryan family, his three brothers having been killed. The captain finds Private Ryan and the captain is mortally wounded. As he is dying, he tells the private to be a "good man" in his lifetime.

Wow. What an effect that had on me. Just the simple statement "be a good man." I needed to do a homily on simply being a good person. Being a good person these days is not a given. There are lots of deadbeat dads and a few moms as well. There are people out there who would rather do you harm than help you. If you don't believe me, buy a cup of coffee for a police officer sometime and listen to him or her. You'll see.

So I wrote a homily about being a good person that

talked about the dedication and the strength it takes to be a responsible mom or dad, to go out every day and do what they do. One of the things I wanted to highlight was that we don't salute ordinary people who just keep doing good a little bit at a time. For a dad who has had a rough day, or a mom who is at the end of her rope because of traffic coming home from her job, it takes real courage to sit down with a son or daughter and read them a story when all the parent wants is a little peace and quiet and maybe a cold beer or a glass of wine. These are the real heroes out there in our society. We all know a few people who fit this description and we sort of just take them for granted. When they die, we don't say enough to celebrate their dedication and devotion.

I wrote and re-wrote this very special homily and I am at a point where I am just now becoming comfortable with it. I may make a few small changes in it, but basically I think it says what I want to say. I hope it salutes the ordinary folks I know who lead ordinary lives and contribute in a very unordinary way to the positive aspects of our culture and society.

Having it Together

I try to live my life in an organized manner, but sometimes I do some dumb things. This is a story about one of those times. Quite simply, it was just a regular nursing home visit – about a half dozen senior ladies to visit, spend some time with, and distribute the Blessed Sacrament. I said hello to the nursing and LPN (Licensed Practical Nurse) staff, and then started my rounds.

I entered one resident's room and started to inquire about how things were going in her life. I smiled when I saw the new sign on her wall that said, "You got to be a tough old bird to make it in a place like this." I had a real survivor there. I opened my pyx and guess what? It was empty.

I excused myself and beat a hasty retreat to my car. I drove to the nearest Catholic Church and went up and rang the doorbell. I had my deacon ID card in my hand to identify myself when the priest answered the door.

I explained my situation to the priest. He said, "You did what?" I told him again, and he invited me in and walked me to the chapel in the rectory. I filled my pyx and thanked him again. He said to me, "Tell me again your name so when I see your pastor I can tell him what a dunce he has for a deacon."

That is the end of the story, but to this day I never open the car door to visit a nursing home without checking to make sure I have enough consecrated hosts.

Misinformation

Sometimes I can go a whole week without hearing some misinformation about the Roman Catholic Church. Most of the time it is trivial. That is no problem, but the story I am about to tell you really bothered me because of its result.

As a Roman Catholic Deacon/Pastoral Assistant, I have always tried to relieve the priest of some of the paperwork by being available to complete the Freedom to Marry form. That is a required form for most, if not all, dioceses in the United States. Someone who knows the bride or groom presents the form and certifies that, as far as they know, the bride or groom is in fact free to marry.

A mom called and asked for an appointment to complete the Freedom to Marry form and I set up a get-together at 2:00 in the afternoon. She was there right on time and we started the procedure. She completed the form and as I was putting the seal of the church on the document she said to me, "You know, Deacon Tom, I have not been to the sacraments in over 20 years." I put the seal down, sat back, and waited for her to go on. She continued, "I am divorced, you know."

I waited and I waited and finally I said, "Is there anything else you want to tell me?"

"No," she said. "When my husband divorced me I spent my time raising my two girls and keeping my good job. This form is for my oldest daughter. She is marrying a real nice man."

"Missis," I said, almost knowing what she was going to say, "Why have you not received the sacraments in over 20 years?"

She replied, "My mother told me that a divorced person could not receive the sacraments."

I swallowed and said, "After the divorce, did you remarry?"

"No," she said. "Raised the girls and tried to be happy as a single mom."

Under my breath I was saying, "Dear Mother of God, talk about misinformation. This poor lady has been living under a presumed cloud of unfounded guilt."

I asked her if she was pressed for time and she said she was not. I got on the office intercom and asked if there was a priest available to talk to me and was told the assistant was there. When he answered, I asked him if he might be available to hear a general confession. He asked for details and I told him her story. He said, "I'll grab a purple stole and be right over."

After introductions, I left and went over to the church and got a small pyx and came back, knocked and was admitted. I administered the Blessed Sacrament. What a moment! Even Father was a little choked up.

I was so pleased to have been a small part of this process of getting this lady with some heavy-duty misinformation squared away. I asked her to come see me after Mass on Sunday when she and her two daughters would be there receiving communion together.

I love it when a plan comes together!

Holy Smoke

It is just a good thing that half the fire fighters in Denver, Colorado are Catholic because if they were not, the church where I was a deacon would have been in a lot of trouble.

It was Holy Saturday and we did the fire thing. Since I live in the foothills, I was asked to bring in kindling and wood for the fire. We lit the Pascal Candle from this fire and we also blessed new holy water. All the folks were outside, the catechumens were in front of the deacons and the priest. It was dark and the wind shifted. The smoke blew into the vestibule and set off the fire alarm.

What followed was a horror story. The constant tone fire alarm sound was only amplified by the screaming sirens of the Denver fire department that showed up with three fire engines and hook-and-ladder. The fire department concluded that there was no fire and respectfully requested that the alarm be turned off. Only one problem – no one knew how. It was decided that the only person who knew how to turn off the fire alarm system was the custodian, so the fire department dispatched a vehicle to try to locate the custodian.

In the meantime, we continued the Holy Saturday service. The people scheduled for baptism or profession into the church walked in. The doors from the vestibule had been shut and the organist tried to play loud enough to drown out the fire alarm buzzer. It was black as pitch in the church. The procession walked down the center. The deacon, carrying the Pascal Candle, chanted "Christ our Light."

Holy Saturday ended as it was supposed to. The catechumens were baptized into the Roman Catholic Church. Those baptized Christians from other Christian denominations made a profession of faith. We were back on track, not on schedule.

When it was all over, the priest, his deacons, the servers, all lectors, and in general all those many lay people who made this work, took a collective breath of relief. It had been a great experience. The new folks needed to be congratulated, the readers needed to be told they read good, the servers told thank you, and above everything else, as tired as all were – smile.

Church is supposed to be fun. Now I know a lot of old pre-Vatican folks will not agree with me, but I challenge you. I think Jesus was kind of a smiley guy in his public ministry. I somehow don't see a lot of folks walking all that way to follow a guy with a frown on his face. I can, in my mind's eye, see him walking up that hill to talk to 5,000 people and saying to himself, "Boy, did I pick a bunch of deadbeats. I chose a bunch of fishermen, the tax collector, a doctor, one I know already will disavow me three times, and one who will betray me. What a crew. But it's the best I can do under the circumstances. Father, can you give me any help?" Of course there is no answer.

After every Holy Saturday service as I drive home, I always have the same reaction. I am just so proud to be a Roman Catholic.

Deacon at Mass,
Assisting a Blind Priest

Recently my pastor called me and asked me if I would care to be deacon of the 5:30 Saturday evening Mass since I had a private baptism following Mass anyway. That way I would not have to come back on Sunday to assist at the 11 o'clock Mass. I said sure. Then Father told me that he would not be the celebrant, but a visiting priest would be. And, "By the way, the priest is blind." "The priest is what?" I exclaimed. "Blind," he repeated. I had no idea that there were any blind priests.

I drove from Conifer to Evergreen thinking to myself, "Okay Tom, how is he going to distribute communion? What if he falls? How will he consecrate – from memory or will he have a Sacramentary in Braille?" I was getting a little nervous. And, I had a baptism following Mass . . .

Father was in his 60's, a Jesuit from Omaha, Nebraska with a wonderful sense of humor and a real spiritual presence. He vested while talking to me about what he would like me to do for him. I made mental notes about any special need he might have. Yes, he would distribute communion. Yes, he had a Braille Sacramentary. He would like me to escort him to the front of the altar for him to deliver the homily, and assist him back to his seat at the end of the homily. I hosts in the tabernacle, and sat down. At that point, I realized that I was totally drenched in perspiration. My shirt was stuck to my back, my alb was stuck to my shirt, and I probably was giving off some not too fragrant odors.

The concluding prayers were read from Braille and I gave the dismissal. I assisted Father to the altar where we reverenced it. I then helped him to the front and down the two steps of the chancel. We bowed towards the altar and, with Father on my elbow, made our recession. We spent the next ten minutes shaking hands with parishioners. People just wanted to touch him and thank him for being there. Many remarked that his homily was directed specifically to them and they thanked him for his wisdom.

was to prepare the altar and receive his gifts, then come get him for the offertory.

Before the first reading, he had a few comments about what we were going to hear; same thing for the second reading. I asked him for his blessing before I read the Gospel. When I was done, I got him and led him in front of the altar where he began his homily. I was really getting concerned because if he tripped and fell, I could not get to him in time.

The guy gave a great sermon and the congregation never took their eyes off of him. I became acutely aware that I was privileged to be part of something very special that Saturday evening. I brought him back to his chair and the collection was taken. The altar was prepared, and I escorted him to it. He began mostly by memory and the rest from the Braille Sacramentary. I felt a lot of emotion building up inside me during the consecration. It was really special to be there with this priest, assisting him, being another set of hands and his eyes. This was so special. It was like I imagined it must have felt for the apostles at the Last Supper

At communion, I helped him get in the best position to handle the folks in line. Then I went to the other side to distribute the Blessed Sacrament for my side. I finished my side and noticed his side was still twice as long. I realized that many people were in line to receive communion from this very special priest. I simply waited until everyone had received from Father and then took the ciborium and assisted him back to his seat. I cleansed the vessels, reposed the remaining

After Mass, when I was outside shaking hands, I found Harold and asked him if he would like to be the first person to receive communion every Sunday. He asked how that could be. I told him at the Lamb of God an usher would tap him on the shoulder and escort him up. He would be the very first person to receive every Sunday. He got a big smile on his face and shook my hand. "Deacon," he said, "we got a deal."

From that day on, every Sunday like clockwork Harold would be number one in line. He would give me a robust "amen," and I would be good. No shaking. No problem.

Amen

During my formation for the diaconate for the diocese of San Angelo, Texas, I was assigned to Sacred Heart Parish in Abilene because I lived there. I was assigned to assist at the Mass at 9:00 a.m. on Sunday. My job was as a Lector and to assist in the distribution of the Blessed Sacrament.

I had a problem distributing communion. My hand would shake. I knew people could see my hand shake. I tried having a bowl of corn flakes with lots of sugar, but my hand still shook. I went on sick call at the Air Base and told the doctor my problem. He prescribed a tranquilizer, but my hand still shook. I was really getting desperate.

One Sunday toward the end of the communion line I saw a senior citizen walking down the aisle. He was a retired farmer impeccably dressed in a nice tan suit and a gleaming white shirt and tie. His face was rosy and clean shaven. His facial tan stopped at his forehead because, as a farmer, he wore a ball cap and he would only get sunburned part way up.

When he got close to me, I said, "The Body of Christ," to which he responded, "amen," only he just did not say a plain "amen." He said an "amen" that could be heard in the church basement. You know what? My hand stopped shaking. The moment I realized my hand was not shaking anymore, I knew I had found the answer to my problem. Now, how do I capitalize on it?